Big Truck's Road Adventure

Written by Amelia Marshall

Illustrated by Dan Bramall

W

FRANKLIN WATTS

LONDON•SYDNEY

All the trucks are ready
at the start of the day.
Engines are **HUMMING**,
tyres turning away.

Flicker, flicker, flash,
the headlights shine bright.
BRRM, BRRM, BRRM,
the trucks move out of sight.

VROOM

VROOM! VROOM! VROOM!
Big truck is on the move!
Its shiny steel wheels
are **fast**, **round** and **smooth**.

Big tanker truck is
WHIRRING and **WHINING**,
its long metal body is
SHIMMERING and **SHINING**.

BEEP BEEP

Car transporter
juggles a heavy load,
BANGING and **CLANGING**
along the busy road.

Dump truck races off
carrying all the waste.
HURRY, HURRY, HURRY,
it speeds in haste!

TOOT! TOOT! Log truck trundles down the track, **heavy** logs of timber carried on its back.

15

Gleaming, **dazzling** rig,
shiny, red and bright,
RUMBLING down the road
all day and all night.

Long yellow crane truck
SWINGS its hook to and fro,
bumping and **bouncing**,
it's always on the go!

19

Chug! Chug!
It's road train — the
longest truck of all,
TUGGING its trailers
in a long, slow crawl.

Speedy tow truck
is **DARTING** and **DASHING**,
racing to the rescue,
orange lights flashing!

CRUNCH

MUNCH

Rubbish truck **CRUSHES** and **SLUSHES** the waste. **Munch! Crunch!** What a funny taste!

WHOOSH, SWOOSH, SWISH!

Delivery truck goes past,
rushing to deliver mail,
it travels really fast!

Whooosh

27

Clink, clunk, clunk!

It's starting to get dark.
The trucks are slowing down,
they need a place to park.

Flicker, flicker, flick,
the headlights fade away.
The trucks have all shut down
until another day.

Truck terms

Wing mirror – allows the driver to see what is behind.

Cab – where the driver sits.

Tyres – help a truck to move fast and grip the road.

Headlights – lights at the front of the truck.

Bumper – helps protect the truck in an accident.

Exhaust – a pipe to let out gas from the engine.

Grille – vents to allow air in to keep the engine cool.

Bull bar or **Roo bar** – extra metal bar at the front of the truck.